HOR

HOUSE

"Feel how cold my fingers are!"

"Wow!" I said, for her hands were polar-bear cold and, when she touched me, the coldness seemed to move through me like frost.

As I began shivering I realized that the front door was open slightly and only a few steps away, so I shoved Jenna through it and stumbled after her. Another second and we were both standing outside on the step, blinking in the sunshine.

We took some deep breaths, and Jenna spread her arms wide and turned her face up to the sun. "That was horrible," she said.

"But what actually *was* it?" I asked. "What happened?"

She shook her head. "I don't know," she said slowly, "but it's not just this damp business. Something's wrong in Horror House. Something's *very* wrong. . ."

Look out for:

Haunted House
Plague House

HORROR HOUSE

MARY HOOPER

SCHOLASTIC

Scholastic Children's Books,
Commonwealth House, 1–19 New Oxford Street,
London, WC1A 1NU, UK
A division of Scholastic Ltd
London ~ New York ~ Toronto ~ Sydney ~ Auckland
Mexico City ~ New Delhi ~ Hong Kong

First published in the UK by Scholastic Ltd, 2004

ISBN 0 439 96398 2

Printed and bound by AIT Nørhaven A/S, Denmark

10 9 8 7 6 5 4 3 2 1

CHAPTER ONE

"I don't believe it," I said. "How could you just walk by that football and not chip it over to me?"

"What?" said Jenna, looking distracted.

"I said, how could you. . ." I began, and then groaned. "Oh, never mind." And I sprinted past her and cleverly flicked the ball up and knocked it towards the sign on the village green reading No Ball Games.

I despaired of my sister sometimes, I really did. How could someone who was my twin not be interested in football? How could *anyone* not be interested in football? OK, she was a girl but even girls like the game these days. I'd been thinking about it and what I reckoned was that if there were such things as footballing genes, then I'd got her share as well as my own.

I ran to the ball and flicked it up into the air. As I did so Jenna said, "Jake. Did you feel anything strange just now?"

"Nah." I shook my head, intent on doing keepy-uppies. My record was twenty-five and I was hoping to break it. "What sort of strange?" I puffed.

"Something. . . Something in the air," she said.

"What sort of something? A smell? Dog's muck?"

"No." She shook her head. "Not a smell. Not that. . ."

"Twenty-two . . . twenty-three. . ." I counted, but then I lost control of the ball, slipped up trying to retrieve it and ended up flat on my backside.

I gave Jenna a little more of my attention because, although she's useless at football and anything else of that nature, sometimes she can sense things. Ghosts-and-spirits type things. And though it sounded mad, we'd encountered quite a few of them since we'd come to live in Bensbury. There was good news and bad news about living in this place: the bad news was that I had to go round with my sister because here I was Billy No-mates, the good news was that instead of mates I had ghosts. I mean, we'd thought that it was going to be the quietest, most boring village in the world, but we'd discovered all sorts of strange goings-on: a ghost dog, a skeleton in a trunk and a very spooky girl from the seventeenth century – and that was just for starters.

"So it's not a smell, then. A vision?" I asked hopefully.

She shook her head again. "Not exactly. More a . . . a presence."

"What's that when it's playing football?"

"A slight . . . tiny . . . wisp of something, that's gone before you can pin it down."

"A person?"

She frowned. "I think so. Someone hurrying towards us. Urgent. Rush. An accident. . ."

"What?"

"Those are just the feelings that are coming to me."

I looked all round and tried very hard to sense something. I couldn't, though. All I could sense was Mrs Hugo – better known as Mrs Huge-o because of her size – pounding across the green towards us. She was wearing an orange frock with flowers all over it and looked like a small landscaped garden.

"Try and ignore old Huge-o, close your eyes and see if you can sense anything else," I said to Jenna. "We're a bit short on spooks at the moment."

"Young boy! You there!" Mrs Huge-o called over to me.

I pretended not to hear her.

"Here, boy!" she said.

"Are you speaking to me?" I asked. "Or is there a dog in the vicinity?" I muttered.

"Yes, you. Doesn't that sign say, No Ball Games?"

"Yes, I do believe it does," I said ultra-politely. If you use this tone to speak to crinklies it throws them completely.

"Well, er . . . what time does your mother's shop close?" she boomed with a voice to match her size.

"It's already closed," Jenna said. "It's half-day today."

"Oh, what a terrible nuisance! Oh dear, oh dear!" she said, sighing as if she'd been without food and drink for a month. "Well, will you go in and ask her if I could possibly have three packets of chocolate biscuits?"

"Not fat enough?" I asked under my breath.

"What did you say?" snapped Mrs Huge-o.

"Not *fast* enough!" I said swiftly. "Ha ha! You weren't fast enough to get over here before we shut, were you?"

Jenna nudged me, reminding me that we're not supposed to be rude to customers *under any circumstances*. "I'll see what I can do, shall I?" she said to Huge-o politely, and she ran back across the green towards our shop. The shop was the reason we'd all come to live in Bensbury: Mum runs it, and a small post office as well, and we live in a flat over the top.

Huge-o stood her ground, pretending I wasn't there, and I pretended she was two opposition players putting up a defensive wall and dribbled the ball round and round her while she alternately tutted, sighed, shook her head and did the "young people today" bit.

When Jenna got back with the biscuits, saying they could be paid for the next day, Huge-o tried to pretend they weren't for her but for a Women's Institute meeting that afternoon.

"Oh yeah," I said as we watched her fat form retreating across the green. "A likely story. Bet that's just her afternoon snack."

"You are so rude," Jenna said.

"So is she!" I retorted. "Calling 'Here boy!' to me as if I was a dog."

"Mum says we've got to be polite to everyone," Jenna said. "She says that the shop needs every customer it can get."

"I'll be polite to them if they're polite to me," I said. I flopped on to the grass. "But never mind about them," I said, "what about this spooky presence you felt. . .?"

She shrugged. "Oh. It's gone now. It was nothing. Probably just my imagination."

"Hmmm. . ." I said, wishing I could spook-spot as well as she could. If I had our share of footballing genes, though, Jenna had most of the psychic ones. She could spot a spook at forty metres.

I did spot someone coming towards us, actually, but this was someone alive and well and going by the name of Mrs Horseface Hall. This, of course, wasn't her real name, but one that Jenna and I had made up. We'd given nearly everyone in the village nicknames according to what they looked like or what they did, just to help us remember them. Horseface – well, yes, unfortunately she did look like one. We also had Bumface Butley, Squeaker Squires,

Stuffer Starr and a whole load of others.

"Horseface Hall fast approaching from the right," I said to Jenna. "Let's go!"

"Where to?" said Jenna. "Where *is* there to go?"

"Oh – let's just go to the dog pound," I said. "Anywhere where we won't have to talk to a wrinkly." And we dashed off before Horseface could try and speak to us.

We'd discovered the dog pound only recently. It was just a walled square, no roof or anything, at the back of the Unicorn pub. It was where, in the olden days, they used to round up stray dogs and shut them in so they couldn't go worrying sheep. A notice on the door said something about this.

"*Worrying sheep*..." I said to Jenna as we went in. "I rather like that expression."

She nodded. "Yeah. Like you can imagine a dog going up to a sheep and saying, 'Your fleece is a horrible grey colour and looks a sight.'"

"Or, 'I've heard you're going to be roast lamb at the end of the month.'"

"'I don't like you and I'm not talking to you any more!'"

Laughing, we slammed the wooden door

behind us and, the walls of the place being just about as high as a goalpost, I began bashing my football towards the end wall scoring imaginary goals. After about fifty or so bashes I got bored, though, and sat down next to Jenna on the bench.

"Want me to try and teach you the offside rule?" I asked hopefully.

"Get off!"

"Go on. Think how handy it'll be when you're watching *Match of the Day*. You'll be able to shout at the ref with me."

"I don't watch *Match of the Day*."

"Well, you ought to." I took a deep breath. "I might as well tell you anyway." I cleared my throat: "*The offside law holds that a player is offside when the ball is played forward to him and he is in the opposition's half of play. . .*"

"Oh, do shut up," Jenna said, and then, just as I was about to carry on regardless, we heard a voice from out of nowhere say, ". . .*and he is standing in a position where there is no defender closer to the goalkeeper than the attacking player. . .*"

I jumped up. "Hey!" I shouted. "Who said that?" The dog pound was hardly big enough for us and a bench, let alone for anyone to hide.

I pulled at the door but it was stuck, so it took me a couple of moments to get outside. Once out, I ran straight round the dog pound looking for whoever it was. There was no one about, though. Jenna came out and she looked too, and then we went back inside.

"Whatever was that about?" she asked.

"D'you think it was a ghost?" I asked hopefully. "The one you sensed earlier?"

"Don't be stupid," she said. "Ghosts don't go round telling you the offsye-drule thing."

"*Offside rule!*"

"Or whatever it is."

"No, but wouldn't it be great if they did," I said.

"So who d'you think it was? One of the wrinklies?"

"Do me a favour!"

"Mr Tragic throwing his voice?" Jenna suggested.

I groaned. "Could be. . ." Mr Tragic was a conjurer and magician who lived on the other side of the green. He called himself Mr Magic but he was actually very *tragic*, forever getting eggs out of your ear or coins out of your nose. He was good at throwing his voice – as I'd discovered when I'd heard a scarecrow talking. "It didn't *sound* like him, though," I said. "I thought it was a girl."

"He does imitations as well," Jenna said. "Anyway, it's probably not a ghost, but let's think that it is."

I nodded. "Yeah! It's about time we had a new ghost to hunt. And a ghost who was a football fan would be *great*."

CHAPTER TWO

"Open the door for Mrs Snape, please, Jake," Mum called across the shop to me the next day. She smiled smarmily. "Thank you so much for your order, Mrs Snape. I'll let you know when it arrives."

Mrs Snape – that is, Snotty Snape, so called because of the almost permanent drip on the end of her nose – gave a mighty sniff and looked at me, waiting for me to leave my place behind the counter, go to the door and open it for her.

Sighing under my breath, I did so. Mum had a thing about me opening the door for customers, as if our shop was Harrods or something. I think she'd have actually liked me to be wearing a green uniform and a shiny hat. She nodded at me now, and frowned, so I flung open the door with an exaggerated flourish and bowed very low as Snotty went out.

"Many thanks for attending our humble shop, your Snottiness," I said as soon as the door was closed behind her.

Jenna giggled, but Mum said, "Jake! Don't talk about our customers like that."

"Well, you make such a fuss of them," I said. "I mean, next time a customer comes in I'll lie down on the floor so that they can wipe their shoes on me, shall I?"

"What a good idea," Mum said. She moved over to the post office counter and started checking down some sort of list, while I wandered over to my favourite part of the shop, the chocolate biscuit section. "You know," Mum said after a few minutes, "we're not doing too badly considering we haven't been here long, but there are new people in Horare House who haven't been into the shop yet. *Or* used the post office."

"You don't say," I said, yawning.

"Who are they, then?" Jenna asked.

Mum ran her finger down the list. "They've got a bit of a name: Mr Ulysses Farrington-Ocelot and his wife, Marjorie."

I burst out laughing. "What stupid names!" I said. "Utterly cranky. I know what we can call them, though."

"How can you? We haven't seen them yet!" Jenna said.

"Mr and Mrs Ulysses Farrington-Ocelot – they're the UFOs!" I said.

Mum started laughing.

"You're right!" Jenna said.

I grinned. "Of course."

Later, once we'd heaved a few crates around and stacked a few boxes, we helped ourselves to some packets of crisps and some rolls and stuff and went outside. That was probably the only good thing about having a shop – you could feed yourself from the shelves. Mum, mind you, was quite strict about what we were allowed to have. I'd have had chocolate flakes for every meal if it had been left to me, and Jenna would have had fudge fingers, but that wasn't allowed, of course.

"So, OK, we've got two small mysteries to think about," I said, squashing crisps into my mouth. (I could almost get a whole packet in at once.) "First there's the . . . um – what did you call it? – *presence* you felt. And then there's the mysterious disembodied voice."

"Oh, please!" Jenna said, looking at me in disgust.

"What?"

"How am I supposed to *sense* things with you sitting there stuffing crisps down your face. Your cheeks are bulging like a hamster's and you're *covered* in bits."

"Nice," I said, but I wiped my hand across my lips and pushed in a few stray chipples. "Is that better? Can you feel anything now?"

"No, I can't," she said. "I usually only feel stuff when I'm not expecting it. It kind of comes up and surprises me."

"Well, think about something else then," I said. "Don't think of ghosts at all. Put ghosts right out of your mind. Don't let yourself dwell on ghosts. I mean, let ghosts be the last thing. . ."

"Oh, do shut up."

"OK, I'll leave you sitting here not thinking of ghosts. . ." I said cheerfully, and I flicked up my football and gave it a mighty kick across the green.

It was such a brilliant, cross-field kick that it disappeared. Went completely out of sight.

"Good shot!" I roared to anyone who might be

listening. "Excellent shot!" I started off after the ball, thinking it had gone into some old biddy's garden. There are rows of twee cottages all round the green, each with a little walled garden in front of them, but when I got to where I thought my ball had ended up, it wasn't there.

I looked all round. It had to be *somewhere*. And then I saw a figure crouching down just behind Stuffer Starr's front garden wall.

"OK, who are you and why have you nicked my football?" I said.

The figure moved and a face beamed up at me. It was a chubby face framed by curly hair in bunches tied with pink ribbons.

I studied her carefully. There weren't any girls in Bensbury; we knew that. There weren't any kids at all. But she looked too sturdy and substantial to be a ghost; I mean, she was probably only about eight but there was no way *she* was a wispy presence. "You'd better get out of there," I said. "That's Stuffer Starr's garden."

"Who's he?"

"It's not who he *is*, it's what he does," I said. "Like, he stuffs things: foxes and dogs and birds and anything he can get his hands on. And then he puts them in glass cases."

The girl gave a scream and leapt over the garden wall. She was wearing a white dress with frilly bits all round the hem, and a pink fluffy cardigan. I don't know much about girls' clothes but I do know Jenna wouldn't have been seen dead in that outfit.

"I wasn't going to keep your ball," she said, handing it back to me. "I was just having a joke."

"Never joke with a Premiership superstar," I said. "I suppose it was you who parroted the offside rule yesterday?"

She nodded.

"So where d'you learn that, then?"

"From my brother. He's fifteen."

"Is he with you?" I asked, suddenly excited.

She shook her head. "I'm staying here with my grandad and grandma, but Jay's gone to stay with one of his mates."

I scowled. Just my luck. Just my luck for *him* to go away and for *her* to come to Bensbury.

"Is that your sister?" she asked, looking across the green towards Jenna.

I nodded.

"Is she nice?"

I grunted.

She gave a pathetic sigh. "I haven't got anyone to play with."

"We don't *play*," I said witheringly.

"I bet your sister would like to play. . ."

"I bet she wouldn't."

But, undeterred, the girl was already making her way towards Jenna while I trailed behind, making *what could I do?* gestures in response to Jenna's *what've you bought her over here for?* ones.

"I'm Claire," she announced.

"That's nice," Jenna said in an uninterested voice.

"And I'm staying here for two weeks of the summer holidays."

Neither of us said anything to this. She was much too cringe-makingly girly for me – she was even too girly for Jenna – and actually, it was only the fact that she knew the offside rule that got me to stay within a mile of her.

"My grandad and grandma moved here a little while ago and this is my first visit to their new house," she said.

"So who are they, then?" I asked, wondering which particular set of wrinklies she belonged to.

"They're Mr and Mrs Farrington-Ocelot," she said, and Jenna and I burst out laughing.

"What's so funny?"

"Well, your grandad's name is Ulysses, right?" I said.

She nodded.

"So they're the UFOs!"

The girl frowned. "So?" she asked. "What's funny about that?"

"UFO! Unidentified Flying... Oh, never mind," I said.

Jenna was thinking about something else; I could see it written all over her face. "So your gran and grandad live in Horare House, do they?" she asked after a moment.

Claire nodded.

"It's a really big old place, isn't it?"

Claire shrugged. "I suppose so."

I knew now what Jenna was getting at. "Is it haunted?" she asked.

"'spect so," Claire said. She smoothed down her flouncy frock and sat down on the ground between us. "So, what shall we play?"

"I told you – we don't *play*," I said.

"So, what *do* you do, then?"

I wouldn't have said a word about it, but Jenna has a bad tendency to blurt things out without thinking of the consequences. "We hunt ghosts," she said.

Claire turned her nose up. "I don't think that's a very good game." She stood up. "Don't you like dancing? Dancing is much better than ghosts. I like ballet and country and hip-hop. What do you like?"

Jenna and I just sat there, gawping at her.

"I do classes," Claire went on proudly. "I've got cer-stifficates for my dancing. I'll show you some of my display pieces if you like. There's one where I have to dress up as a dear little robin and. . ."

"Actually. . ." Jenna began.

". . .we'd rather eat live bees than watch you dancing."

"And we've got to do something for our mum at the shop!" Jenna finished, and she and I ran – no, sprinted – back there as fast as we could.

CHAPTER THREE

"Just my luck," I groaned, back at the shop. "Just my luck that the only visitor under forty in the village turns out to be a *girl*."

"Well, I don't like her either," Jenna said, pulling a disgusted face. "I don't want to do dancing where you dress up as a robin and I don't want to *play* with her. She'd have me playing tea-parties with dolls."

"Who's that you don't like?" Mum asked as she stacked packets of soap powder. "Who're you talking about?" And then she said to me wheedlingly, "There's about forty of those foil sachets of cat food in a box on the floor there – many more than we need. Will you put them up on to the top shelf for me? You'll need to get the small ladder."

Ignoring the ladder, I picked up the sachets and began to hurl them two-handed from behind my head. "And another brilliant throw-in!" I yelled as each one left me.

"Do you *have* to be so noisy, Jake!" Mum said, holding her ears. "And if they get spoilt no one's going to buy them. Anyway, who was that you were talking about?"

"Just a girl called Claire – she's the granddaughter of the Farrington-thingies," Jenna said.

"She means the UFOs," I said between brilliant throw-ins.

"Really?" Mum asked. "Is she living with them?"

"Only for two weeks," said Jenna.

"Two weeks is long enough," Mum said. "If you make friends with her and she starts coming to the shop, that'll be enough to get them coming and establish them as customers. Is she your age?"

"No, much younger," Jenna said.

I threw in my last tin. "And she's a wuss," I added.

"Never mind about wusses – whatever they are," Mum said. "You just try and make friends with her. Why don't you invite her over for tea."

"Per-lease," I said.

As Jenna and I exchanged horrified glances, Mum went through to our back room. "I'm going to put the kettle on, make a cuppa and have a five minute sit down," she said. "I'll come and deal with anyone who wants something from the post office if you two look after any shoppers. OK?"

We said it was, and I helped myself to a small chocolate biscuit which had unaccountably got knocked off the counter during the Great Cat Food Throw-in.

Jenna wandered over to the shop door and looked out. "This is so *boring*," she said, "and we're not going to get many customers this morning because the wrinklies don't come out when it's raining."

I glanced out of the door myself. "What're you talking about?" I said. "It's not raining. It's not even *nearly* raining."

Jenna looked outside again and her eyes widened. "Oh, no. It's not. . ."

"Then why did you. . .?" I stopped. I could feel something too. Something, a *feeling*, coming through Jenna.

She stared outside with wide eyes. "It seems to

me that it's raining outside, lashing down, and a woman is coming across the green. I think there's been an accident. She's crying, she's got a cut on her forehead and there's blood running down the side of her face."

"Go on," I said, knowing this was probably the same figure that Jenna had seen earlier. "What's this woman wearing?"

"A long, pale yellow dress with lace down the front and the back caught up in a bustle – like Victorian ladies wore."

"Anything else?"

"She's got long white gloves halfway up her arms."

"Yes?" I asked encouragingly.

"The rain is coming down harder now and it's mingling with the blood on her face and falling on to her dress leaving long red streaks . . . and her gloves are getting covered in blood. . ." Jenna was speaking quickly now, taking quick breaths between sentences as if she was doing the running instead of some mystery woman.

"Go on," I said, checking outside again to make sure I couldn't see anything. Sometimes I could – but often I just sensed things through Jenna.

"Well, she's crying and she's trying to run quickly but her dress is trailing on the ground and holding her up, and her satin shoes are covered in mud."

"Where's she going? Is she heading to one of the cottages?"

"No, she seems to be coming here. . ." Jenna gasped then and shook her head, as if to clear it. "She's gone! Someone's *really* coming across the green now and the woman's disappeared."

I glanced outside and groaned as I recognized the figure on the far side of the green. "Oh, no. It's Claire!" I said. "Little Miss UFO."

Jenna didn't react to this for a moment, but rubbed her eyes and shook her head as if to clear it. "Phew!" she said.

"*That* was more than a wispy presence, wasn't it?"

She nodded, shivering slightly. "That was more like a full-blown ghost."

I passed her the last bit of my chocolate biscuit. "Can you remember any other details?"

She frowned. "Well, I seemed to see a big tree and . . . and I somehow got the feeling that it was involved in the accident. Maybe . . . maybe her carriage hit the tree and overturned, and she was thrown out."

"It was definitely a Victorian woman?"

She nodded.

"Well, let's go over to the library sometime and look through the old newspapers. We can see if there were any accidents in Victorian times – any coaches overturned and passengers killed."

"There must have been *loads* during that reign," Jenna said. "Victoria was on the throne for *ages*."

"But there can't have been many accidents round here, surely? And we can ask Ratty – she might know something," I said, because Ratty Ratcliffe, even if she was half-woman and half-rodent, knew loads of stuff about the history of the village.

Claire, shopping basket over her arm, was almost at the door of the shop. "Oh dear," Jenna said, "here she is, all ready to *play* with us. . ."

"I bet that basket's got a miniature tea set in it," I said as I dashed forward and turned the sign on the door to CLOSED.

She pushed open the door regardless.

"Sorry!" I said. "We're just about to close for the day."

"You're not," she said, sticking out her bottom lip. "It's only four o'clock."

"Jake's right – we're closing due to . . . to lack of staff," Jenna said.

"But *you're* here," she pointed out. "Both of you."

"Not for much longer. We're just about to. . ."

"Is everything all right?" Mum's voice called from the kitchen where, obviously, she'd been watching and listening.

"Fine!" I called back.

"You'll have to serve her now that Mum's seen her," Jenna hissed in an undertone. "She'll go mad if you. . ."

And of course Mum then appeared, smoothing down her overall and smiling smarmily. "Oh, you must be Miss Farrington-Ocelot," she said. "How lovely. How are your grandparents? I haven't had the pleasure of meeting them yet."

"Very well, thank you, and I've got a big shopping list here from them," Claire said importantly. "But Jake says that. . ."

"Jake says he'll be very pleased to serve you!" I said quickly.

Mum gave me a look, and insisted on staying in

the shop until she saw the shopping safely into Claire's basket. After that, she went back into the kitchen, leaving us with a big cardboard box to put all the extras in, which meant that Jenna and I were needed to help carry the stuff back to Horare House with Claire.

I tried to get out of this, suggesting that Jenna should go on her own, but she wasn't having any of it. The matter was still under discussion when Claire said, "Oh, I've been asking about ghosts, and our housekeeper says there are loads and they live in the west wing."

We digested this news.

"Are you sure?" Jenna asked.

"Yes. Honestly! So when we get back with the shopping, we can go and look for them."

I looked at her, suspicious about that "we". The last thing I wanted was a kid with a frilly dress and hair with ribbons interfering with our ghost-hunting activities. But my sister OK'd it before I could say anything.

"It's a deal!" Jenna said. "We carry your shopping home and you let us see round the . . . er . . . west wing."

Claire nodded happily. "And then we can all play ghosts together."

There was a moment's silence.

"Now see what you've done," I muttered to Jenna.

CHAPTER FOUR

I took my football over to Horare House with me. I believe, if you're a really keen player, you should never go far without your football because you never know when a scout from one of the big teams will turn up.

I carried the box of groceries and dribbled the ball, and as I dribbled I also asked Claire some searching questions to see how much she actually knew about football. What she actually knew, though, was *nothing*. Zilch. When I started talking about the offside rule she just repeated what she'd said before, parrot fashion, without actually understanding a word of what she was talking about. Still, I thought, what could you expect of a girl? Especially one with curly bunches.

About half a mile out of the village we turned into a long, winding drive lined each side with fir trees. I realized that although we'd gone past the entrance a few times, we'd never actually seen Horare House as it was tucked away and hidden behind trees.

"So about this ghost," Jenna began as we started up the long gravel driveway.

"*Ghosts*," Claire said. "Ghostses. Lots of them."

"What sort of ghostses?" Jenna asked.

"All sorts."

I looked at Jenna and rolled my eyes. I didn't believe a word of it. Talk about a false ghost chase.

"Did the housekeeper say anything about a lady in a long yellow dress?" Jenna asked.

"Ummm. . ." said Claire. "I think so."

"What other ghosts?" I asked.

"Oh, all sorts. Ghosts rattling chains and going *whoooo* and carrying their heads under their arms!"

"Oh, that's good," I said sarcastically. "That's just the sort we like. You mean like the ones in *Scooby-doo*?"

She nodded. "That's it! That's exactly right."

She smiled at us, bunches bobbing as she walked. "And if we don't find ghosts we can play something else, can't we?"

Obviously, I thought, we weren't going to find anything. It was a good job I had my football with me or the whole afternoon would have been a complete waste of time.

The house, though, when it came into sight, seemed to loom up over us in an awesome way. It was a towering great thing built of dark grey stone, with about eight windows on each side of a large, studded black door. There were little towers at each corner and as we got closer I could see there were ugly carved stone heads in a line above the top windows, each face staring blankly into the distance. Why anyone – even some old Farrington-thingy – would want a house as big as this, though, I couldn't imagine.

"Are there just the two of them? Why did your grandad want a house *this* big?" Jenna said, picking up on what I was thinking. Or maybe I'd picked up on what she was thinking before she'd had a chance to say it.

"Oh, he said he might open a school," Claire said. "He had one in London."

Jenna and I didn't know what to say to this, so

we just made faces above Claire's head. Kind of *oooh-err-get-you* faces.

There was a big old bell outside but Claire just pushed open the front door and we followed her in. She rushed off and Jenna and I stood looking around us. The hall was as big as a football pitch and tiled in black and white squares, with a great swooping central staircase coming down the centre and two suits of armour standing like they were on duty beside the bottom stair. It was quite dim in there because there was only one window at the back, made of stained glass, and it all looked dusty and gloomy.

"If ever a house should be haunted, *this* should be," Jenna said, her words echoing round us.

"Bet it isn't, though. Bet she just said that to get us here."

Jenna closed her eyes briefly. "I'm not sure," she said. "I'll need to be here a bit longer before I can say for definite. There's something strange here," she sniffed, "and it all smells odd . . . damp . . . as if things are decaying."

"Well, we'll try and find out a bit. . ." I began, and then we heard Claire calling, "Come on, you two!" from somewhere out the back, so, still carting all the groceries, I parked my football and we followed the voice to a jumbled old kitchen where Mr and Mrs UFO were waiting for us.

If, after seeing the house, I'd had time to wonder what he – Mr UFO – was going to be like, I'd have pictured him with a long black beard and a cloak, someone tall and spooky and mysterious. And Mrs UFO would be like a witch.

They weren't, though; they looked quite boringly tame. They were both thin and small and a bit dusty, and had little wire glasses with round frames. They were sitting at a long old table which was covered in books and papers.

"Ah, Claire's friends bearing provisions!" Mrs UFO said, as I hunted for enough space to put the stuff down on the table.

Jenna introduced us both and they said something cringe-making, like they were pleased that Claire had found some playmates, and then Jenna said the bit about Mum sending her regards and hoping to see them in the shop very soon.

"Jake and Jenna have come here to see the ghosts," Claire said.

Mr UFO looked up from a big leather-bound book. "Which ghosts are those?"

"The ones Mrs Scudder told me about," said Claire.

Mr UFO looked at his wife. "Who's Mrs Scudder, dear?"

"She's the housekeeper," Mrs UFO replied.

"We know Mrs Scudder," I said, nudging Jenna. Scatty Scudder – called that because she was – used to be a housekeeper for Mr Doddery Dudley, who'd owned Wellington the ghost dog. It had been seeing Wellington which had first alerted us to the fact that Bensbury was alive with ghosts. (Or I suppose that should be *dead* with ghosts.)

"I think all the ghosts are in the west wing," Claire said.

"Ah. Yes. They would be," Mr UFO said, winking at me. "The west wing has been shut up for years and years and we've only recently opened it."

"Do you know, the last people to live here only used two rooms," Mrs UFO said to us, "and when they left, the house was empty for fifteen years."

"So is it all right if we go and play in the west wing?" Claire asked.

"Yes, off you go and play your games," her gran said, while I sighed to myself. I *knew* we weren't going to find anything good. . .

* * *

The west wing was stuffed with old furniture. Iron beds were piled in one room, another held nursery furniture: a rocking horse and some high chairs and cots, and another just seemed to be a furniture depository for the rest of the house, with any amount of old stuff piled high and covered with white dust sheets. It was cold in these rooms, and smelt musty and old, but we didn't exactly see anything you'd call spooky.

"So where were these ghosts seen?" Jenna asked Claire.

"I thought you'd know that," she said reproachfully. "After all, *you're* the ghost hunters."

We didn't say anything to this, but Jenna began to walk about touching things and standing quietly in different parts of the room, trying to absorb the atmosphere and see if there were any vibes to be picked up.

"What's she doing?" Claire asked.

"Ssshhh!"

"Is she playing ghosts?"

I glowered at her. Other people – like, strikers taking penalties when I'm in goal – have trembled before that glower. She didn't even seem to notice it, though.

"Can I play ghosts as well?"

"No, you can't!" I hissed.

Jenna walked around a bit more with Claire trailing along behind her, arms outstretched like a cartoon ghost. I walked around a bit too, but couldn't feel anything strange.

"I don't *think* there's anything here," Jenna said after some moments. "At least, not in this part of the house."

"Exactly what did Mrs Scudder actually say about ghosts?" I asked Claire.

"Can't remember."

"Is she around?" Jenna put in. "Can we ask her ourselves?"

Claire looked vague. "I think it's her day off. But anyway, we can *pretend* there's ghosts here, can't we? We don't have to have real ones to play."

I gave her the look again. The glower.

"We *do* have to have real ghosts," Jenna said to her nicely, "because we're real ghost hunters."

"Yes, but. . ."

"And we've got to go home now," she added.

"But if you want us to waste a whole afternoon some other time," I said, "just let us know."

"All right!" said Claire, the sarcasm going right over her head.

"We'll go and talk to Ratty," I said to Jenna as we made our way back down the big staircase and I picked up my football. "She'll know if there's ever been any ghosts here."

"And I bet she'll know about my Victorian lady as well."

"See you tomorrow, then!" Claire said to us at the door.

"Not if we see you first," I muttered.

We looked back at the house as we walked down the drive. It looked dark and sinister and I, for one, wouldn't have wanted to go to school there. "Never mind about Horare House," I said. "It looks more like Horror House to me. . ."

CHAPTER FIVE

Ratty Ratcliffe stood at her front door, her pointed nose quivering slightly, her beady eyes looking at us like a rodent eyeing up two pieces of cheese.

"Now," she said, adjusting the moth-eaten bit of fur around her neck. "You asked me about Horare House. What do I know about its history? Let me think. . ." She was quiet for a moment, and then she said, "Of course, you do know it was a school back in the olden days?"

We shook our heads.

"It took boarders, boys from aged six upwards. It was a school right up until the end of the Second World War, I believe."

Jenna and I exchanged glances. So that was

why it was so suitable for old UFO to turn into a school again.

"Mrs Scudder said something about a ghost," I put in encouragingly.

"Well, *ghost* may be overdoing it a bit. I think there was a certain atmosphere about the place that people objected to, that was why it took an awful long time to be sold. And there was something about the rooms being damp. . ."

"Damp! And was there a decaying smell?" Jenna asked.

"Yes, I believe there was, and though one of the potential buyers had a survey done to try and discover why it was so damp, no particular reason was found." She adjusted the ratty neckpiece. "Lots of people came to look at it over the years but no one was really interested until this new lot. The Farrington-Ocelots – such a ridiculous name!"

I grinned. "And because his name is Ulysses. . ."

". . .we call them the UFOs!" Jenna giggled.

"*Do* you?" asked Ratty, looking at us curiously. "Why's that?"

"Because they are Unidentified. . . Oh, never mind," I said.

Another moment went by with Ratty still thinking and us still standing there. "So you haven't heard about any ghosts there, then?" Jenna said after a while.

"Not really. At least, not one that has actually materialized and been recorded."

"What d'you mean by that?" I asked.

"Well," Ratty said, "I'm not a believer in ghosts and ghouls and things that go bump in the night, but I do believe that sometimes . . . sometimes a place can retain an image of a traumatic happening."

"Ah," said Jenna, as if she knew exactly what Ratty was getting at.

"And I also believe that some people have the power to see and recreate such traumatic happenings," Ratty went on.

"You mean, like, *psychic* people?" Jenna asked, nudging me.

Ratty nodded. "Exactly. I'm not a bit psychic myself – I only see what's put in front of me, but other, more sensitive, people may have walked around Horare House with a view to buying it and sensed that something wasn't quite right about the place." She smiled and her beady eyes went into slits. "Now, if there's nothing more. . ."

"Oh yes, there *is* something else we wanted to ask," I put in quickly. "Do you know anything about an accident near here in Victorian times? A coach overturned?"

"And a woman killed?" Jenna asked.

Ratty shook her ratty head. "Again, nothing springs to mind. I'll have a look through my scrapbooks, though. And you could go and look at old newspapers in the library. The local ones are always a good source of village news."

We said thanks, and then she went indoors and we sat on her wall to think about stuff.

"What d'you reckon, then?" I asked Jenna. "Is there anything going down at Horror House, or is Claire just giving us a load of pants?"

"I'm not sure," Jenna said. "There might be something in it. That damp business . . . I definitely felt that."

"Yeah, but damp is just that. *Damp*. It's got nothing to do with ghosts, has it?"

"I don't know," Jenna said.

I heaved a sigh. "These new ghosts are being a bit tricky. We can't seem to get going on this one *or* the Victorian one."

"Let's do what Ratty said and go and look at some old newspapers in the library, then."

* * *

Mr (Fishface) Fichard was in charge of the library. He had a shiny bald head, rather protruding eyes and a gaping mouth like a goldfish, and he seemed to be there whatever day you chose and whatever time you went in.

I asked him for Victorian newspapers – there had been a local weekly paper back then – and of course the first thing he asked was which year we wanted.

"Not sure," I said.

"We're researching for a school project," Jenna said, which was what we always said when we were doing ghost research. "It's a project about. . ."

"Transport!" I said quickly. "Transport in Victorian times. How safe was it and were there any bad accidents round here?"

"That's a very *large* sort of project," Fishface said, but he started looking through some cupboards behind him and eventually pulled out a couple of bundles of old newspapers. "I'll let you have them year by year from when Victoria came on to the throne," he said. "Otherwise you'll disappear under a sea of newsprint."

Luckily, the papers weren't very thick; about

eight pages, and quite a lot of the space was taken up by advertisements.

"We'll look for carriage accidents," I said, "and anything else of interest. Maybe we'll find something about Horror House."

And so we started looking. And we carried on looking. We started with 1837 then went on to 1838 and 1839. We looked and looked until my eyes glazed over and Jenna slumped down on the desk, practically asleep.

"Let's blow the whistle," I said finally. "I've had enough and we've only got through three years. We'll come back another day."

Jenna yawned hugely and loudly and Fishface stared over at us with his big goldfish eyes.

"I'm *starving*, as well," I complained. "They ought to have a tuck shop here."

Jenna struggled into a sitting position and pinched her cheeks to wake herself up. "Look, we're into 1840," she said. "Let's just get to the end of this year."

Groaning, I picked another paper off the pile. Wearily I opened it and just as wearily glanced down the page . . . and then I saw it. Nothing about a ghost, but something *very* interesting all the same.

It was an advertisement filling up half a page. There was a picture of Horror House at the top and underneath it read:

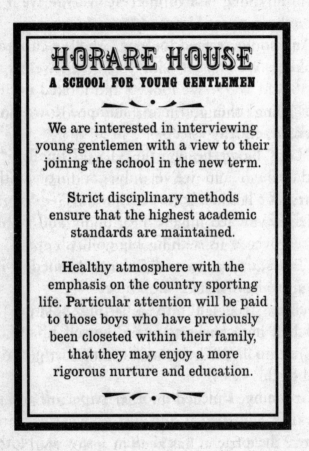

> **HORARE HOUSE**
>
> **A SCHOOL FOR YOUNG GENTLEMEN**
>
> We are interested in interviewing young gentlemen with a view to their joining the school in the new term.
>
> Strict disciplinary methods ensure that the highest academic standards are maintained.
>
> Healthy atmosphere with the emphasis on the country sporting life. Particular attention will be paid to those boys who have previously been closeted within their family, that they may enjoy a more rigorous nurture and education.

Excitedly, I showed the page to Jenna. "Look at this: Horare House!"

She read it. "I bet it wasn't very nice there. . ."

"Hmmm. Dunno about that – it mentions the sporting life. See, they had the right idea – lots of sport! I wouldn't have minded going there."

"It wouldn't have been football and rugby," said Jenna. "It says *country* sporting life."

"So?"

"Killing things, in other words. Shooting rabbits and trapping deer and all that."

"Oh," I said. I didn't fancy that.

"And look at that last bit – about rigorous nurture. I bet it was one of those hearty outdoor schools where you had to get up in the middle of the night and go running to toughen you up, and where they got you to march up hills carrying a piano on your back."

"Hmm," I said. "Maybe I wouldn't have wanted to go, then."

Jenna shivered. "No, I don't think you would. . ."

And so we finished the year and went home.

"Your little friend has been in to see you!" Mum said as soon as we got our noses around the door of the shop. "She said something really exciting has happened and she wants you to go up to Horare House straight away!"

Neither of us moved.

Mum clapped her hands. "Off you go!" she said. "What are you waiting for? And you, Jake, remember to say to Mr and Mrs Farrington-Ocelot how very much I'm looking forward to seeing them, and that I hope their plans to open a school go well."

"I suppose you told her that. . ." I muttered to Jenna.

"A new school in the village would be very good news," Mum went on. "Think of the groceries they'd need!"

Jenna pulled at my sleeve. "Come on, we might as well go," she said and, groaning, I allowed myself to be dragged outside again without even having time to stuff my pockets full of biscuits.

"You never should have told Mum he was going to turn it into a school," I said to Jenna. "She's just going to go on and on about it."

"Oh, never mind that now," Jenna said. "Maybe something *ghostly* has happened. . ."

CHAPTER SIX

No one came when we rang the bell at Horror House, so we just pushed open the door and went through into the hall. We looked around for a bit and I investigated one of the suits of armour and thought – as I always did – that it'd be murder to wear and however did you go to the loo?

We called "Hello!" loudly but no one appeared, so we made our way through to the kitchen where Mrs UFO was sitting in exactly the same place, behind the same jumbled pile of old papers and books, as she had been before. The only difference was that she appeared to have a tea cosy on her head.

"Hello!" Jenna said, making her jump. "We've come to see Claire."

"Claire?" Mrs UFO asked, looking as if she'd forgotten she ever had a granddaughter. "Claire. . ." she said thoughtfully. "Oh yes, I remember. She said to tell you to go along to the nursery in the west wing."

We said thanks, and Jenna nudged me to say the piece I'd promised Mum. "Oh, and our mum sends her best wishes and looks forward to seeing you and hopes your plans to open a school go well," I rattled off quickly.

"Yes. Your mother. Of course." Mrs UFO smiled at us with a bemused look. "And your mother is. . .?"

"Our mother runs the post office and grocery shop in the village," Jenna said.

"Ah, groceries," said Mrs UFO. "Mrs Scudder deals with foodstuffs. I have nothing to do with them at all. The written word –" she gestured to the battered old books in front of her – "these are my foodstuffs."

"Are they to do with the house?" Jenna asked tentatively.

"That's right, dear. There's a register for every year the school was opened, matron's records, a punishment book and all sorts of things waiting to be catalogued and itemized. We discovered them all when the west wing was opened up."

"You'll have to talk to Rat – Mrs Ratcliffe," I said. "She runs the history society in the village."

"Ah yes," she said vaguely, adjusting the tea cosy. She opened one of the heavy books, turned to a page and said, "Do you know that a boy was once put in leg irons for a week because he didn't eat his dinner? And another was made to go into the village just wearing his pyjamas and a dunce's cap?"

Jenna and I began backing away. She was clearly loopy, and would fit in very well with the people of Bensbury.

We climbed the stairs and turned left into the west wing, then started going in the rooms one by one, Jenna calling Claire's name and me maintaining a superior silence.

No one appeared.

"Where *is* she, then?" Jenna asked.

"Maybe she's gone into a time warp," I said, then added, "I wish."

"I expect she's hiding. Playing hide and seek or something."

There were oil paintings all along the passageway and I stared at them. They were all the same type of thing: a grumpy-looking old man holding a scroll, wearing a black gown and a flat thing on his head. An inscription underneath the one I was looking at read: *Gilbert A Strong. Headmaster from 1845–1860. Of course*, I thought as I moved down the line of them. *That* was why all the paintings looked similar, they were of school headmasters down the years: same pose, same scroll of paper, same black gown and mortar board. Only the faces and the type of facial hair were different, according to what the fashion had been at the time: full beard, small moustache, long sideburns, neatly trimmed beard and so on. None of the pictures were the sort of thing you'd want on your wall at home and it was no wonder they'd been shut up in the west wing along with all the other junk.

There was one in particular I didn't like the look of *at all*, and I stayed staring at him while Jenna went into the last room. His eyes were a steely, penetrating blue, and he had long furry sideburns which joined up with his thick moustache. He was smiling – but not in a nice having-my-picture-painted way, but so that he looked sly and devious. His inscription read: *Oliver Connington. Headmaster from 1915–1921.*

"What d'you think of him?" I asked Jenna

when she came out of the room. I felt I could sense something quite sinister and thought it would be interesting to get her take on him.

She glanced at the picture and shuddered. "I think – *evil*. He would have been a beast of a headmaster."

"Exactly what I thought," I said.

We looked again, then we both shivered at the same time and turned our backs on him.

"No sign of Claire, then," Jenna said as we walked down the corridor.

"No. So why bother to get us here if she's going to put in a no-show?"

We walked back towards the staircase, and were just about to go down it when we heard a movement from one of the rooms behind us – a kind of rhythmical thudding on the bare floorboards – and we began to retrace our steps.

"What do you think?" I asked Jenna. "Does it feel like anything spooky's happening?"

"Nope!" she said, shaking her head.

The noise, it turned out, was coming from the room with the old nursery furniture in it, and was caused by the battered rocking horse lunging backwards and forwards. We may have been taken in very briefly – for about half a second –

and then I jumped forward and put my hand on its mane to stop it rocking. Jenna then bent down and snapped the length of thread that was attached to the front of the rocker – which went in a direct line towards a small white-painted wardrobe standing against a wall.

We looked at each other and both put our fingers to our lips, then began to creep towards the wardrobe.

"Wow!" I said loudly. "The rocking horse is moving on its own."

"Amazing!" Jenna said. "It must be possessed by a ghost."

"That's what I reckon!"

"I should think it's probably one of the most frightening ghosts ever."

"You bet! It's utterly evil . . . the most utterly evil ghost ever to have –" I grabbed hold of the wardrobe door as I spoke – "ridden on a rocking horse!" I said as I flung the door open to reveal Claire hunched inside.

She stared up at us. "Hello, Claire," I said. "Doing anything interesting?"

She pursed her lips.

"Oh, I see," Jenna said. "We rushed over here because we thought you needed us, only to find you sitting in a wardrobe pulling a rocking horse on a piece of cotton."

"You've taken us away from our *proper* ghost-hunting activities," I said sternly.

She pulled a sulky face. "Well, now you're here we can play ghosts. One of you can hide in the wardrobe and I'll pretend to. . ."

"No," I said. "You can stop right there."

"We're going home," added Jenna, and she and I walked back towards the stairs with Claire trailing after us making whining and whimpering noises.

We'd just reached the staircase when we heard a terrific crash from down below and, looking over the banisters, saw Scatty Scudder flat on her face with a mop on top of her. An overturned bucket was nearby and there was a large puddle of water all over the black and white tiles.

We ran down the stairs and helped her up. She looked just as scatty as usual – scattier, in fact – with her hair sticking out like twigs from a rook's nest.

"Silly me!" she said. "I tripped over the mop!"

This, if you knew Scatty, wasn't any sort of a surprise.

"Oh, bless!" she said, looking from me to Jenna. "It's the twins."

We scowled at her.

"Mrs Scudder," Claire said, hopping from one foot to the other. "Tell them about the ghostses."

"Whatever d'you mean?" Scatty asked, water dripping from her overall on to her shoes. Which were odd, I noticed. One brown and one black.

"She means the *ghosts*," Jenna explained. "I think you said something about this house having some ghosts."

"I never did!"

We all looked at Claire. "Well, it was something like ghosts," she said.

Scatty frowned. "I might have said something about *them*," she said, pointing at the suits of armour. "I might have said that they looked a bit spooky standing there like there was someone inside them. That's all, though."

We looked at Claire again and there was a long silence. "Well, that's nearly ghosts," she said.

Jenna and I didn't even bother to say anything, just gave her a withering look each. Scatty picked up her bucket and mop. "Well, I must get along," she said.

"And we're going too," I said to Claire.

"Please don't ask us to come again," Jenna added, "not unless there's a real ghost."

Sulkily, scuffing her feet, Claire followed Scatty towards the kitchen, while Jenna and I made for the front door. We'd almost reached it when Jenna suddenly stopped dead, shuddered and wrapped her arms around herself. "Oh, so cold!" she said.

"*What?*"

"It's really intensely cold just here!" she said, her teeth beginning to chatter. "Can't you feel it?"

I closed my eyes, trying hard. "What? D'you mean like a gust of cold air or something?"

"More than that . . . there's a . . . an icy feeling right through me. It's like being out in the snow." She pushed her hands at my face. "Feel how cold my fingers are!"

"Wow!" I said, for her hands were polar-bear cold and, when she touched me, the coldness seemed to move through me like frost.

As I began shivering I realized that the front door was open slightly and only a few steps away, so I shoved Jenna through it and stumbled after her. Another second and we were both standing outside on the step, blinking in the sunshine.

We took some deep breaths, and Jenna spread her arms wide and turned her face up to the sun. "That was horrible," she said.

"But what actually *was* it?" I asked. "What happened?"

She shook her head. "I don't know," she said slowly, "but it's not just this damp business. Something's wrong in Horror House. Something's *very* wrong. . ."

CHAPTER SEVEN

"What's clear," I said to Jenna the following day, "is that we've got two potential spooks here."

"Or at least, spooky happenings."

I nodded. "Correct. We've got the Victorian woman and we've got something in Horror House."

She shivered. "Definitely something in Horror House. And – seeing as we both felt it – possibly something connected to that headmaster."

"To the evil Oliver Connington. Yeah, I reckon he must have something to do with it as well," I said, pleased to have had the same sort of feeling about him as Jenna had. "The thing is, how are we going to investigate anything properly there with Claire around?"

"Dunno," Jenna said, shaking her head.

We were in our kitchen at home chatting about this, so didn't know that the shop was filling up until Mum called for one of us to go and help her. Jenna and I held a short debate – well, a row, actually – over whose turn it was, which ended up with us both yelling at each other and then Mum calling that we could jolly well *both* come and help now. Immediately.

Opening the door into the shop, we found it full of star-turn crinklies: Bum-face Butley, Gibbon Gibbs, Piggy Pinder, Stuffer Starr and – worst of all – Mr Tragic. It was pension day, so all the top village names were there.

On seeing us, Mr Tragic moved swiftly to Jenna's side. "Ah, my lovely young lady assistant!" he said, acting as if he were on stage. "Just step forward, my dear, and show the rest of the customers that there is nothing up your sleeve."

As Jenna was wearing a sleeveless T-shirt there obviously wasn't anything. The rest of the crinklies, having seen this act probably four hundred times before, didn't even bother to look over.

"Now, look under your arm and what do we

see!" With a flourish Mr Tragic stepped forward and removed an egg from Jenna's armpit. "Keeping it warm so that it would hatch, were you? Ha ha!" he said, laughing loudly at his own wit.

He turned to me. "Now, young man," he said, getting some cards out of his pocket and fanning them in front of my face, "would you be kind enough to choose one of these cards? Don't tell me which one!"

I shot a look at Mum. A *get-me-out-of-here-quick* look.

"Oh, Mr Adams!" Mum said sweetly, calling him by his real name.

He turned to her and bowed. "Do call me Mr Magic, Madam!"

"Well . . . er . . . Mr Magic, I've called the twins in here so they can help in the shop, and we're so busy that they won't be able to assist you with your magic today. Sorry!"

"Well, never mind," he said jovially. He had a gaping smile and teeth big enough to eat you. "Perhaps you could magic me down a nice tin of corned beef from the top shelf instead!"

"You go and magic yourself to the back of the queue!" said Bum-face Butley, red in the face with indignation. "You've only just got in here!"

And so the fun-packed day went on and we were busy in the shop for quite a lot of it, with only a short lunch break when I was allowed outside to scoff rolls and have a bash at my keepy-uppies, which by sheer persistent genius I managed to get up to a record total of thirty.

Jenna did manage to ask Squeaker (she squeaked rather than spoke) Squires, who looked to be about a hundred years old and who'd been living in the village since the Dark Ages, if she'd ever heard of a headmaster at the school called Oliver Connington. She squeaked back that she remembered when Horare House had been a school, but the village people had never mixed with the boys or teachers so she'd never known any of the staff by name.

How were we going to find out more?

The answer to that came around four o'clock when Claire appeared outside the shop with a basket over her arm.

Seeing her on the doorstep, Jenna and I both ducked down behind the counter to hide, but Mum, who was in the post office section, called across to us that our friend was outside and we were to come out at once.

"We *know* she's here, Mum," Jenna said, as we reluctantly appeared.

"That's why we're hiding," I added.

Claire came in (wearing a frilly, fairy-on-the-Christmas-tree dress) and then Mum really went into overdrive as, a moment or two later, Mrs UFO came in as well.

We had to endure a whole load of "Welcome to the village" and "I hope we'll be able to obtain every footstuff you need" malarkey and then, when Mum had finished wittering on about fresh local produce, Mrs UFO announced that she and her husband had to go to London on urgent business that night.

"I wondered if your two children could come over and keep Claire company," she said. "Mrs Scudder will be staying the night too, of course, and cooking the children a light supper, so if they'd care to –"

"We can have a midnight feast!" Claire put in.

Jenna and I looked at each other and rolled our eyes.

"Well!" Mum said. "What a treat for you!"

"Treat!" I said, then made the sort of strangled

noise you'd make if your team had conceded two injury-time goals after being one up the whole match. "Look," I went on, "there's no way that. . ." And then I thought about what I was about to turn down. We had the chance to be in Horror House *all night*, on our own apart from Scatty (who hardly counted) and would have masses of time to investigate spooky happenings.

Jenna nudged me and I knew the same thought had occurred to her. ". . .no way that we'd ever turn it down!" she finished my sentence.

"No. As you say, a real treat," I said, smiling smarmily at Mum (who'd been expecting trouble and looked astonished).

"Hurray! It's a sleepover!" Claire crowed. "You're coming to a sleepover and we'll have a midnight feast!"

"Yes," I said. "Fantastic."

We left the shop in good time that afternoon because we'd decided to go to see the vicar on our way. He knew lots about the village, and he'd helped us before, with deaths and dates and stuff. Besides, he had a bit of trusty left foot and it was ages since I'd had a kickabout with anyone any good. Or anyone at all, come to that.

I gave my football a whack across the green then ran up to it and waited for Jenna to catch me up. She was ages doing so – and when I looked back she was just standing there with a soppy look on her face, so I went back to gee her up a bit.

"Come on!" I said. "If we're going to see your Reverence or whatever his name is we ought to get going."

Jenna just stared at me blankly.

"What's up? You look as if you've –" I stopped. "You *have*, haven't you?"

She nodded slowly. "It was her again."

"Who?"

"Who d'you think? Minnie Mouse? The ghost of the Victorian woman, of course. I came through the shop door and then saw that it was all damp and rainy outside. I turned to go back and get my mac and then I realized that it wasn't real rain, but just . . . just like it had been before."

"The rain was an illusion?"

She nodded. "And I knew I was going to see her again. So I just stood there and she came across the green, crying – like before – coming from that direction –" Jenna pointed over to the right where the main road was – "and I could visualize a big tree in the distance, and knew that her carriage or whatever it was had crashed into it. I couldn't see these clearly, I just knew they were there. I could see *her* all right, though."

"And could she see you? I mean, did she look as if she wanted to tell you something?"

"I'm not sure. She just seemed to be running and blundering about a bit, as if she couldn't see properly because of the rain and because she was crying. And there was this blood from her head running into her eyes. . ."

I pulled a face. "What else? Was there anyone else around – like a coachman?"

Jenna shook her head. "I didn't see anyone."

"And what about around here?" I gestured around the green, thinking it would be good to get an idea of how long ago this accident had taken place. "Did it look the same then as now? What about all the cottages?"

"I don't remember anything about those," Jenna said. "At least, nothing sticks out as being different, so I think everything must have been more or less the same in those days – whenever it was. The only really distinct thing was her."

"Hmm," I said, and I was puzzled because although it was a cert that Jenna was more psychic than me, I was usually a *bit* psychic. Why hadn't I seen anything of *this* ghost, then?

CHAPTER EIGHT

We stood there until Jenna thought she'd recovered from the psychic business. Then she said there was something she wanted to do before we went to see the vicar.

"I want to go and look over there..." she pointed across the green to our right, ". . . where that woman came from. She seemed to come from the direction of the main road and I'd like to try and find the tree that I saw in my mind."

"OK," I said as we set off. "What sort of tree was it? A particular make of tree? Willow? Oak?" I frowned as I tried to remember any other trees. "Lava-tree . . . ha ha!"

She pretended she hadn't heard that. "I think it

was an oak." She spread her arms. "Yes, I think it was what they usually refer to as a mighty oak: big wide branches, very broad and old."

"Was it green?" I asked.

"Of course it was green," she said crossly, "what d'you think it was – blue?"

"Cool down, sis," I grinned. "It might have been bare."

"OK, I see what you mean," she said. "No, it had masses of leaves."

"So at least we know that the accident happened sometime in the summer," I said.

"Yeah. We just don't know *which* summer."

We went across the green, skilfully avoiding Moaning Mowlem, on her own so for once not moaning, and Slaphead Slade, his bald head glinting in the sunshine. I was kicking my ball along in front of us, and Jenna was carrying a rucksack with our overnight things. We'd also brought, on Mum's insistence, some stuff for a midnight feast. These were mostly of the chocolate variety and I intended to eat them as soon as we got there, because I didn't reckon that Scatty's so-called supper would be up to much.

When we got close to the main road Jenna dropped the rucksack and ran the last few metres towards a big tree which had heavy branches dangling almost to the ground. "This is it!" she said, looking up excitedly. "This is it as I saw it. It flashed into my mind . . . this exact shape!"

"Are you sure?"

She nodded. "Positive." She pointed up at a branch. "This big section coming out here which swoops down in an arc . . . I saw it all."

I went up to the tree and looked at the bark closely, running my hands over it.

"This is no time to start tree-hugging," Jenna said.

"Don't be mad. I was looking for marks."

"What – marks caused by the accident? You wouldn't get those after all this time, surely?"

"Why not?" I said. "People carve their initials on trees and they stay for years. If it had been a really big smash then there might still be a scar on the trunk where the carriage had gouged into it."

She came to stand beside me and looked up. "And is there?"

"No," I admitted.

We were still standing there staring at it when I thought of something and groaned.

"What's up?" Jenna asked.

"You said that this tree is exactly the same as the one you saw in your vision. . ."

She nodded. "That's right."

"Don't you see, though: if this tree has been here since Victorian times it's something like a hundred and fifty years old."

"So? That's nothing. Trees can live for ages longer than that."

"Yes, but they don't stay the same, do they?"

She stared at me for a moment, and then she got it. "I see what you mean! The accident happened in Victorian times so if this *was* the tree, then it would have been much, much smaller back then. More like a sapling."

"Exactly. So it can't be the same tree."

She pulled a puzzled face. "It's so like the one I saw, though. Identical. . ."

"Yeah, but a tree's a tree, isn't it?" I said. "One's pretty much like another one. I expect the one you saw has been chopped down for firewood by now."

Subject closed, I turned round and steadied my football ready to kick off.

Jenna stared at the tree a little more, then she turned her back on it and shrugged. "I suppose you're right."

* * *

The rev wasn't in the church when we got there, so we had a quick look around the graveyard. What, ideally, we'd liked to have seen was a tombstone saying something like: "*Here lies a lady in a yellow dress and bonnet, killed on a nearby road as a result of a carriage accident in 1888*". Also, while we were about it, we'd have liked to discover the grave of someone from the Horror House school who'd been murdered by the evil headmaster, Oliver Connington. Ghost hunting was never that easy, though, and all we found were inscriptions on the tombstones saying "Our Dearest Granny" and "A Faithful Servant" and even these were so mossy and weathered that we couldn't read more than a word or two.

We were just about to leave when I heard the back gate clank open and a booming voice called, "Is that young Jake the ace striker I see? To me, lad!"

I felt a bit nervous about kicking a ball about in a graveyard but the rev did insist, so I sent it flying to him over six tombstones and a marble angel. He caught it neatly on the top of his shoe, steadied as if about to shoot and then said, "No, I'd better not – just in case the bishop happens by."

We went over to join him and he asked what we were up to.

"Well, we're here because—" Jenna began, and before she could blurt out the truth I cut in, "Because we're doing a project!"

"Oh yes?"

"It's about Victorians and their transport," I went on (and as it was in a churchyard I had my fingers crossed).

"We wondered if there were any graves here of women who'd died in carriage accidents," Jenna added.

He scratched his head and the three strands of hair which covered his bald patch flopped over to one side. "There isn't one that springs to mind," he said. "Though I'm sure there *were* plenty of accidents in those days. Horses bolted, carriages went into ditches or overturned, highwaymen asked for your money or your life – the roads were mighty dangerous places."

"More dangerous than a Porsche and a Mercedes speeding round a hairpin bend at 210 miles an hour?" I asked.

"Maybe not," he said. "Especially if you add a Maserati. . ."

"The thing is," Jenna interrupted, "we can't

read most of the inscriptions on the really old gravestones." She put on her most wheedling look, the one she always uses with Mum to get her own way. "D'you think you could possibly have a quick look through your burial records to see if they mention a woman's death as a result of an accident near here in Victorian times?"

He nodded. "I'll have a look for you later. But, you know, just because the accident was nearby, it doesn't mean she was buried here. The mere fact that it was a carriage accident meant that the person was just passing through. If anyone died their body would have been taken back to their own parish for burial."

Jenna and I looked at each other. "We never thought of that," I said.

"There's something else," Jenna said. "D'you know anything about Horare House when it was a school?"

"I didn't go there, if that's what you mean," the rev said jovially. "It stopped being a school in about the 1940s – before my time."

"We just wondered what it was like."

"For another project," Jenna put in.

He grinned at us. I don't think he was at all fooled by the project business but he was too nice to probe. "I do know that it had a very harsh regime," he said. "Schools did, in those days. Haven't you read your Dickens?"

We both shook our heads.

"Well, boys hardly had anything decent to eat, they got strict punishments for the slightest misdemeanour, had school work seven days a week. . . Need I go on?"

"Um. . ." Jenna said thoughtfully. "Would the boys who went to school there have come to this church on Sundays?"

"They would indeed," the rev nodded.

"And be buried here?" I asked.

"Ah! Funny you should want to know that. The thing is, there's a small patch of consecrated ground at Horare House – a little burial plot – which used to surround an old wooden chapel. Sometime during the last century the chapel fell to pieces and it was then that the boys started coming to services here instead. They kept the burial ground going, though, and I believe anyone who died whilst at the school – boys or teachers – were buried in it."

"Where is it then?" I asked. "I mean – front or back of the gardens?"

The rev shook his head. "I wouldn't know

about that," he said, "but it's probably completely overgrown, covered all over in briars and nettles and impossible to get to."

I nudged Jenna. "We'll see about that," I said, because something told me that that burial ground might be quite interesting. . .

CHAPTER NINE

As I'd feared, Scatty's light supper was about as bad as it could be. It consisted of what she called soup, which looked and tasted like hot water with a pea in it, and then cheese on toast. While we were eating it Jenna whispered that she must have raided the mousetraps for the cheese because it was so hard and rubbery that even being melted on toast hadn't helped.

"Rank," I muttered to Jenna.

"Chuck-up city," she muttered back.

Afterwards we had apples and custard and I wouldn't even like to tell you what they looked like, let alone how they tasted.

We ate this "food" sitting at the top end of the long table in the kitchen, Scatty having pushed the piles of books and old papers to one side. I shoved my food around my plate, just grateful that none of my old footballing mates could see me sitting there with two girls and, even more horrifyingly, a big china doll and an earless teddy, each on their own chairs with small pieces of cheese on toast in front of them.

"Isn't this fun!" Claire said, looking from me to Jenna and back again. "It's a tea party!"

We ignored her.

"Is Teddy eating up?" Claire asked, looking at me pointedly. "Could you put something in his paw, please?"

"No," I said shortly.

"Dolly hasn't got anything in her little cup," Claire said to Jenna.

Hard luck. In my head I heard Jenna mutter this, but what she actually said, being politer than me, was, "Oh dear, what a shame."

The funny thing was, Claire didn't seem to care that we weren't playing properly or that we were being so sarky; the mere fact that we were there seemed to be enough for her. I reckoned she was used to it. She had a fifteen-year-old brother, after all.

The evening passed slowly and painfully and it

was only having a pocketful of chocolate biscuits that got me through it. We asked if we could go outside, thinking that we'd try to find the school graveyard, but Scatty wouldn't let us, saying that she'd promised UFO that we wouldn't roam around the grounds because of there being barbed wire and open wells and Other Dangers. While Claire was occupied making herself a pair of fairy wings, Jenna and I had a look around the house again but, apart from us both getting a fit of the cold shivers, and Jenna feeling once that her clothes were wet when they weren't, we didn't encounter anything odd. Somehow, though, we found ourselves back in the west wing, staring up at the portrait of Oliver Connington.

"They do say that sometimes, in a really good painting, the eyes seem to come alive," Jenna said after a moment.

I suppressed a wussy shiver. There *was* something about his eyes: hard, evil, penetrating – all those things. "It's as if his wicked, fiendish qualities are all condensed there," I said.

"And he's looking down through the years and still seeing us. . ."

Abruptly, we both turned away and began to walk back to the main part of the house.

"Do you think," Jenna asked, "that the two things are somehow connected?"

"The Victorian woman and Evil Oliver?" I said. "Who knows?"

"Maybe her son was here," Jenna said thoughtfully, "and she heard he was being bullied or something, and she came to take him home, and on the way her carriage overturned and she died. . ."

"And because she wasn't able to rescue him, *he* died as well," I finished.

"It's possible," she said. "Oh, no! Of course it isn't. She's definitely Victorian and he – Evil Oliver – wasn't at the school then. He wasn't here until – what?"

"1915," I said.

"So they're not connected. And . . . and I just don't get the feeling that they're one and the same ghostly happening, do you?"

"No," I said, not wanting to be left out – though actually I'd hardly had more than a wisp of feeling about the Victorian woman. That ghost seemed to be almost entirely Jenna's property.

There was no TV at the house and, what with Claire trying to get us to play embarrassing games every moment, the evening was a very long one, so when nine-thirty came and Scatty said we'd better be getting to bed, we didn't much mind. It meant we could soon get on with the ghost hunt. . .

Scatty showed us where we were sleeping, which was in the east wing – we turned right at the top of the stairs. Jenna was in with Claire and their room was big and square in shape with horrible red, furry wallpaper. It also had a four-poster bed hung with sagging velvet curtains which (Claire demonstrated amid flurries of dust) could be pulled around to enclose it completely. The rest of the room was filled with old furniture: a wardrobe as big as a small house, an ugly dressing table with a row of Claire's toys on it and a couple of squashy, battered sofas. The lights were dim, everything smelt damp and musty and the whole effect was gloomy enough to give you the creeps.

I was sleeping in the adjoining bedroom and my room, because it was on the corner and L-shaped, was even bigger, with tall windows reaching from floor to ceiling. It had the same sort of stately home furniture as the girls' room, including a four-poster bed, and the same musty, old-church smell, too. I sniffed deeply and pulled a face. A few football posters would have cheered it up, but I didn't happen to have any on me.

Scatty put hot water bottles in our beds (Jenna said she saw the steam rise from the sheets) and then went downstairs, leaving Claire busily occupied with making arrangements for the midnight feast and setting the alarm on her watch for twelve o'clock. "And after we've had the midnight feast we'll all play ghost hunting, won't we?" she said to us.

"Maybe," Jenna replied. She came with me to the bedroom door. "As soon as she's gone to sleep I'll turn off her alarm and come into your room," she whispered.

I nodded. Claire could keep her midnight feast, we were going to have a midnight ghost hunt (and yeah, OK, I was just feeling the tiniest bit frit about it).

The bathroom was right at the end of the corridor and was quite plain and boring, with white, cracked tiles and a cold stone floor. It was so cold in that house, in fact, that I decided to get *more* dressed instead of *un*dressed, and put on my tracksuit bottoms and hoody to go to bed in. As I cleaned my teeth I wondered to myself if it was the same bathroom that the boys had washed in all those years ago, and decided that it probably wasn't. It seemed fairly modern and if Horare House had had, as the rev had put it, a harsh regime, then the boys would probably have just stuck their heads under the cold pump in the yard in the mornings.

I went back to my bedroom and climbed into the huge bed. Despite the hot water bottle the sheets felt cold and clammy, and I wondered how long it was since anyone had slept in them. Faintly, through the wall, I could hear Claire bleating on about something and guessed she was going through some elaborate game with her toys.

I can usually get comfortable and fall asleep anywhere, but that night it was impossible; I just kept shivering with sudden cold fits. I wrapped my arms round myself and tucked my feet under me, glad I'd kept my thick socks on. To keep my mind off the bitter cold, I went through all the Premiership players that I knew.

Time passed. I could feel the dampness in the air – and weirdly, when I looked up, it seemed to be hovering over the bed like a mist. Even the furniture looked strange and menacing in the darkness – as if it was looming up in front of me – so I took my torch from my rucksack and directed its beam across the room, trying to prove to myself that everything was OK.

It had gone quiet next door. Surely Claire was asleep by now? So why didn't Jenna come in? I lifted my head to listen more carefully and it seemed that the house was absolutely silent with a weird kind of stillness, as if it was holding its breath, waiting for something to happen.

Something *horrific* to happen. . .

Those words came into my head and refused to go away, so I began a football chant, softly, under my breath, "*Going up, going up, going up. . .*" over and over again, my teeth chattering with the cold. I wondered about pulling the curtains around the bed, but almost immediately decided not to. If anything was going to creep up on me – the ghost of Evil Oliver, for instance – then I wanted to see it straight away. I shone the torch around the room again, still chanting under my breath, straining to see right to the far end of the room where the beam didn't reach. Was Jenna ever coming in, or had she fallen asleep along with Claire? And what was that little noise in the corner of the room? Something was scratching. A mouse, probably. *Had* to be. . .

Suddenly I was caught by a cold shudder – a

ghost-walks-over-your-grave type of shudder which made me sit bolt upright and flash my torch around the room yet again. *Nothing*. I stayed in a sitting position, though, piling the cold pillows up behind me, and stared into the shadows.

"Is there anyone there?" I said, but my voice sounded so pathetically girlie that I coughed and said it again, louder and bolder. "*Is there anyone there?*"

No answer. No noise at all. Just the mist hovering, and the looming furniture.

My eyelids were drooping when something suddenly caught my eye. Something utterly bizarre: on the wall to the right of the bed I could see a film of water, running straight down from top to bottom, covering the entire surface like a waterfall, shimmering and shining in the torchlight. It was making a soft pattering noise, like rain falling on leaves.

I gave a yelp of fright, leapt out of bed and charged into my sister's room. She was more psychic than I was . . . let her sort it out.

CHAPTER TEN

"Jenna!" I croaked hoarsely, flashing my torch across the girls' room. "You awake?"

"Wha–what's going on?" came her voice, groggy with sleep.

I reached her side of the four-poster in about two seconds. "Quick! You'll never believe it!" I shook her shoulder. "You've got to come and look at this!"

She struggled into a sitting position, then glanced at Claire sprawled beside her, eyes tightly shut. "Ssshhh!" she said. "Don't wake her."

"Never mind about her – come into my room – quickly!"

"Ssshhh. Be *quiet*," she said. She reached across to the bedside table for her torch.

"Why were you asleep?" I hissed. "I thought you were coming into my room."

"I was," she said, "but I waited so long for Claire to fall asleep that I must have dozed off."

"Come on now then. Quickly!"

"Wait a minute." Reaching over to Claire, she undid the wristwatch on her arm, peered at it, then fiddled with the winder. "It's a quarter to twelve," she said. "The alarm will be going off in ten minutes."

"Just hurry!" I said, practically pulling her out of bed.

We ran across the bare floorboards and then paused in the doorway to my room. It was so cold in there that it felt as if we were standing in front of a huge fridge with its door open.

"Brrr. . ." Jenna said, and her breath streamed in front of her like a puff of smoke. "What is it you wanted me to see?"

"Isn't it there?" I asked, hanging back. It wasn't that I was scared to look myself. Well, OK, I was. Just a bit.

She shook her head. "I can't see anything. I can *feel* it, though," she said, shivering. "There's an intense, icy coldness in this room. Horrible. . ."

"Look over to that far wall. Shine your torch

there!" I urged her, and I made myself look, too.

"What am I looking for? A ghost?"

"Just look!"

Our torch beams fell on to the far wall and I saw . . . nothing. I made the beam move slowly across the wall, not knowing if I was relieved or disappointed. "It's gone."

"What's gone? Was it something supernatural?"

"I should say," I shivered. "It was like . . . like a waterfall."

Jenna started laughing even though her teeth were chattering. "Right! A waterfall indoors, coming down the wallpaper?"

"That's right. That's exactly right."

I followed her as she went round the bed and stood by the wall. "There's nothing here now," she said, pressing her hand on the paper. "It feels damp – but no damper than the rest of the house." She shone her torch around. "I must admit there's something very odd about this room though. It doesn't feel right."

"None of this house feels right!"

"But this room especially. . ."

A fraction of the moon showed itself from behind a cloud and sent a silvery light across the room. "Whatever it was has gone now, though. Look," she went on, "d'you want me to stay here with you for a bit?"

"Course not!" I said, pulling a scandalized face. "What, d'you think I need looking after?"

"No, but it might just be better to have the two of us here. I'll stay if you want."

"No, I. . . Well, OK," I said quickly, before she changed her mind.

She went back to get her jacket and then we sat on the bed together, pulling the cover up over us and leaning against the piles of cushions. It was still freezing so I dredged out the hottie but it was lukewarm and worse than useless, and we tried to play I-Spy but neither of us really had our mind on the game. Slowly the moon emerged fully and slid across the window, casting a weird, unearthly light over everything.

"It reminds me of being in the haunted house that night," I said in a whisper, "waiting for the ghost of the murdered bride."

"Don't remind me!"

I suddenly felt incredibly tired. "But nothing seems to be happening here," I said, yawning hugely. "I suppose it wouldn't matter if we fell asleep."

Jenna yawned too. "Yeah. Just let's close our eyes for a moment. . ."

A few seconds later we both heard the noise at the same time, like a gentle pattering of rain. It was a noise that wouldn't have been strange if you'd heard it outside, but was *very* strange inside. In a *room*.

"What's that?" Jenna said in alarm.

"It's happening again!" Not sleepy now, I shone my torch across the wall. Water was sliding and falling in a huge silver sheet right across it.

Jenna, gasping in amazement, drew in a big breath and kind of choked on it, as if she was drowning. She gave two or three of these choking sorts of breaths and, not knowing what else to do, I grabbed hold of her and thumped her on the back, like you'd do if someone had got something stuck in their throat. This seemed to make her breathe normally again and, when we looked at the wall a moment later, the water had disappeared.

I slid off the bed, went over to the wall and put out a shaking hand to where the water had been falling. There was no trace of anything wet.

"No sign of it," I said, baffled.

"You don't say," Jenna said, still breathing deeply.

I climbed back on to the bed. "So what d'you think?" I said. "Weird or what?"

"Very weird indeed," she said, sitting there just staring at the wall.

"The strange case of the weird, watery wall," I said, to try and lighten the mood.

She stayed deep in thought for some moments. "OK," she said. "We agree that this room is haunted, right?"

"Right."

"Although it's obviously not haunted all the time."

I shook my head. "Our presence seems to be making it happen."

"Exactly," she said. "Like Ratty said – a place can retain a memory of a traumatic happening, and some people are able to act as mediums to recreate that happening. We're the link between the thing that happened here in the past, and *now* – the present day."

"But it only seems to show itself when we're off guard," I said, feeling quite pleased that I'd acted as a medium all on my own earlier on. "Like when we were about to fall asleep."

She nodded. "OK. So obviously we don't want to just move out and sleep in another room."

I shook my head. "Nah. We'd never find out what it was all about, then. No, we'll stay here, keep watch. . ."

"But *pretend* to fall asleep at some point," she said. "And then we'll see if this whatever-it-is manifests itself properly."

"OK. But it's going to be a long night," I said. I punched at the pillows to plump them up a bit. "Still, there'll be plenty of time for you to learn the offside rule. . ."

"*A striker from an attacking side is offside when he is in the opposition's half. . .*" she murmured dozily. I prodded her. ". . .*And when he is standing in a position where there is no defender closer to the goalkeeper than the attacking player. . .*"

I yawned. "Go on. . ."

"And when . . . when. . ."

I heard her say that and then felt myself going lollopy and feeling almost warm enough to doze off. When it's three o'clock in the morning, pretending to go to sleep is only just an eyelid's blink from *really* going to sleep. *I'll just sleep for a moment*, I thought. *It won't hurt.*

I could only have been asleep for an instant, just a catnap, but I woke up feeling like I'd been in the deepest of sleeps so that I could hardly make myself come to.

"Wake up!" Jenna was saying in my ear. "Wake up, Jake!"

"What's going on. . .?"

"We're going to drown, that's what's going on. Wake up, will you!" She shook me, pinched my cheek.

"Ow!" I said. "No need for that."

"Look, Jake! Just look, will you?"

I opened my eyes and Jenna shone the torch beam on to the wall where the water was coming down again, smoothly and almost silently.

"*Now look at the floor!*"

I looked down. The lower half of the room was now a shining lake of water. It had risen to about a foot above the floorboards and, where the surface faced the moonlight, was topped off by a line of silver. There had been an old brown rug lying beside the four-poster and it was now floating, coming up to the level of the bed. I gave a yell. "Whaaa? What's happening?"

"Look at that bookcase – and the wardrobe!" Jenna cried, clutching my arm.

I looked over to see that the water had already reached a quarter of the way up the wardrobe. It lapped across the dressing table stool and filled the first compartment of the empty bookcase. At any moment it looked as if the furniture might float away.

"Is the water real?" I asked in disbelief.

"Try it!" Jenna said.

I bent over and, stretching out my right arm, dangled it out of the bed until my fingertips touched the water. I tell you, it felt as if I'd dipped my hand into a bucket of ice. I drew it back quickly. "It's real, all right," I said. "We'd better get out and swim for it!"

"It's trying to drown us!"

There was a confused, muddled few seconds when we tried to disentangle ourselves from the bedclothes in order to plunge ourselves into the water, then Jenna suddenly pulled at my arm again.

"Look at it now! The waterfall's stopped!" She pointed across the room. "And the water's disappearing back to where it came from!"

She was right. The water had now sunk below the first shelf of the bookcase and was moving smoothly down the wardrobe. Another moment and it had receded completely, leaving the brown rug back in its place on the floor.

"Wow!" I said shakily.

"If I hadn't seen it I'd never have believed it," Jenna said faintly.

Neither of us spoke again for some moments, then Jenna said, "I wonder what would have happened if we hadn't woken up? Would we have drowned?"

"And anyway, why d'you think it happened in the first place?"

Jenna looked up to the ceiling. "I kind of think it's to do with something that happened there. In the attics, maybe. . ."

"We'll have a look tomorrow." I looked at my watch. "It's three-thirty," I said. "If we go back to your room now, how long can we have to sleep?"

"At least four hours," Jenna said. "As long as Claire doesn't wake up and want the midnight feast."

CHAPTER ELEVEN

"Teddy wants to say good morning. . ." I heard dimly in my ear.

"Gerroff!" I muttered, sinking deeper into my hoody.

I felt a stuffed toy being bounced along my arm. "Teddy wants to know what happened to the midnight feast. . ."

Blearily, I lifted my head. It was morning and I was stretched out on the four-poster in Jenna and Claire's room, with Jenna slumped beside me, deeply asleep.

Teddy was now being bounced along Jenna's arm. "Teddy wants to wake you up!" Claire sang out.

I rolled over and lay on my back. I remembered

now. I remembered it all: the icy frostiness in my room, the waterfall cascading down the wallpaper and the lake which had covered the floor and risen up the furniture.

"What time is it?" I asked groggily.

"Seven o'clock," Claire said. "Time to get up and play!"

I groaned and an echoing groan came from Jenna. "It's not fair ... I've only just got to sleep. . ."

"What are you doing in this room anyway?" Claire demanded. "And what happened to the midnight feast? Why didn't anyone wake up? Teddy is very cross about that."

"The toys had a midnight feast on their own," Jenna murmured, still half-asleep. "They ate everything."

"They ate all the pies ... they ate all the pies. . ." I muttered.

"I don't believe you!" Claire wailed. "And what about the ghostses? We didn't get to play ghostses."

I glanced across at Jenna. "Well," I said, "we might just do a bit of ghost hunting this morning."

"Oooh, goodie," said Claire. "Let's go down to breakfast now, then!"

* * *

Scatty's porridge doesn't bear describing, let's just say that if the world ever runs out of wallpaper paste I know where they can find a good substitute.

The UFOs were expected home about eleven, so we were back upstairs by eight o'clock, still yawning but dead set on finding out more about what had actually happened in my room – and why.

Claire wouldn't be shaken off (we did our best, believe me) so in the end we had to tell her that yes, we *were* going to play ghosts. Her special part in this was to sit very quietly on my bed, watch what we did and tell us if she saw anything spooky.

Then we tried to forget she was there.

Jenna stood by the window with her eyes closed, all the better to pick up psychic clues, while I applied a bit of logic to the situation.

"The water came from above. Right?" I asked, ignoring Claire's squeal of "What water?"

Jenna opened her eyes and nodded. "It came from above and tried to flood this room. . ."

"So what's *above* this room?"

"It's on the corner!" Claire butted in. "There's nothing above it."

We both looked at her. "Are you sure?" I asked.

She nodded, bursting with the knowledge. "There are servants' rooms on the second floor in the *middle* of the house, but nothing at the corners."

"I'd better just go and check," I said. I ran along the corridor, down the main staircase and out into the grounds, then looked up at the window of my room where Jenna and Claire were waving to me. Then I walked backwards to get a fuller view of the house.

Claire was right: although there were little windows on the second floor in the centre of the building, these got progressively smaller and lower so that by the time they reached the corner they'd disappeared. What my room, and the room on the opposite end, *did* have above them, though, were the little round towers. They could have been merely for decoration – or they could have been *very* small rooms.

I went back and reported to Jenna.

"I bet it's a secret room!" Claire said immediately. "A secret room full of skellingtons!"

Jenna and I exchanged glances. One "skellington" had been quite enough, thank you very much, when we'd found the bride in the trunk.

"I shouldn't think so," I said.

"I hope not," said Jenna. She pointed to the bookcase. "I reckon . . . if there *is* a secret door in this room, that it's about there."

"Have you had a feeling about it, then?"

She shook her head. "It just stands to reason. That bookcase is almost exactly the same size and shape as a door, and judging by the look of it, it's been there for ever. So, say someone who lived in this house knew something dodgy had gone on upstairs – all they had to do was to move the bookcase into place and there was the door: *gone*."

Claire clapped her hands. "Let's move the bookcase away! Quickly!"

"You stay there on the bed," I said to her. "You've got a special job of warning us in case any ghosts appear behind us."

"Or skellingtons. . ."

"Yes. Exactly."

The bookcase wasn't very heavy and the two of us managed to drag it away from the wall quite easily. Behind it was a lot of dust and fluff, a rolled-up newspaper – *and a closed door.*

Someone had removed the door handle so that the bookcase could sit flat against the wall, so I had to go back to my rucksack, find my penknife and work out how to manipulate the lock mechanism and open the door. This took ten minutes or so and we were jittery with impatience by the time the door creaked open and Jenna and I shone our torches into a recess containing a winding stone staircase.

"Just as we thought. . ." Jenna said, and Claire jumped off the bed and pushed in front of us to say, "Wow! A haunted staircase!"

"We don't know that yet," I said.

"I'm going up first!" said Claire. "I'm going up first because it's my house and not yours."

"No, *we're* going up first," I said firmly.

"Because *we're* ghost hunters," Jenna added, "and you're just our assistant."

To tell the truth, I wouldn't have minded someone else going up first and discovering whatever-it-was at the top, but as the only male around I had a reputation to keep up so, with Jenna close behind me, and Claire close behind *her*, I began climbing the winding staircase. It was pitch black and had the same rather revolting musty smell that seemed to crop up all around the house. There were masses of cobwebs, too, and more than once my foot squashed on to something which might well have been a dead mouse. It was too dark to see if there were any spiders, but I was sure there must be any amount of great big ones. The sorts with hairy legs (but I wasn't thinking about those).

At the very top, the stairs opened out on to a small landing and I swung my torch around the space, nervous about what I might see. It wasn't quite so dark here because, cut into the brickwork, was a long slit of a window with no glass.

When the torch beam fell on the big tin bath in the middle of the room my heart skipped a beat. Knowing our luck, it was bound to have a body in it. A *skellington*. My eyes flickered round to Jenna, close behind me.

"You look," she said. "But I don't *think* there is. . ."

Reluctantly, I shuffled forward a few inches and peered into the bath. Phew! No bones – but several contenders for the Spider of the Year contest.

"What d'you think?" I asked Jenna. "What happened up here?" I lowered my voice so that Claire, now making revolting noises about the spiders, couldn't hear. "D'you think someone died?"

She closed her eyes briefly. "I don't think they died, but I think something awful happened to someone . . . to one of the boys who went to school here."

"Really?"

"Something bad happened. Something traumatic which was never acknowledged."

"I wonder if it was a punishment?"

We looked at each other. "Punishment!" Jenna said. "What about that book that Mrs UFO was reading?"

"Downstairs!" we said together.

We went downstairs and found the punishment book on the kitchen table almost straight away. It was a big, black leather book which opened to show pale blue sheets and neat writing across the pages in faded ink. It had dates, boys' names, their "crimes" and their punishments. It also said who was to carry out the sentences.

"I bet Evil Oliver was in charge of the

punishment we're looking for," Jenna said.

"So start looking in 1915," I said, ignoring Claire, who was wittering on asking us what we were doing all the time and why weren't we looking for ghostses?

We turned to that year and went down the page line by line. The crimes were things like speaking in class, not making a bed properly, not remembering every word of a poem or not being sufficiently grateful for food. The punishments ranged from flogging and being put into solitary confinement to being given a starvation diet and being deprived of sleep. I tell you, they made a hundred lines seem like an absolute doss.

There was nothing that even mentioned that little tower room, though, until we got to almost the end of 1916. To December fifteenth.

"Here it is," I said, gasping as my eyes sped quickly along the lines. I read out: *Billy Kingsley, aged ten. For spilling water over his text book. Boy to be kept for one day and one night up to his neck in bath of cold water in the tower room. Mr Connington will oversee.*

"Oh, poor thing – just for spilling some water!" Jenna said, and even Claire went quiet. "It must have been awful. Freezing! Imagine being put in a bath of cold water in that room in December, with no heating and no glass in the window."

I shook my head, trying to think what it must have been like. "And he – Evil Oliver – I bet he kept pushing his head under the water," I said. "Poor Billy!"

"I wonder if he froze to death?" Jenna asked, and then said, "It was . . . like . . . a really traumatic thing, but I don't get the feeling that he actually died up there."

"This book doesn't say anything about what happened afterwards."

"There's another book under here!" Claire piped up. "It says on the front: *Matron's Records*."

I took a deep breath. "Pass it over."

It didn't take long to find Billy. He'd died at the beginning of the following year, 1917.

"*January 2nd. Billy Kingsley, aged ten. Billy died after spending two weeks in the school sanitorium suffering from severe pneumonia.*" I read out. In smaller letters it read: *Following immersion in a cold bath.*

"There!" I said, sitting back. "He died as a result of being forced to sit in freezing cold water for twenty-four hours."

"We were right. Evil Oliver did for him," Jenna said. "It may not have been directly – but he murdered him just the same."

We were quiet for a while. "I wonder how many other kids suffered because of him," I said then. "Talk about a demon headmaster."

Jenna looked at Claire. "Maybe when we tell the UF – I mean, your gran and grandad – what happened, then they'll keep that tower room open."

I nodded. "I think . . . Billy would like that. Maybe he just wants what happened to him to be acknowledged and remembered."

"That's right," Jenna said. "If the room is open again then I think somehow his spirit will be free. You know, like what happened with the bride – she stopped haunting the cottage after we'd found her."

Claire heaved a sigh. "But where *is* he, though? I haven't seen a ghost, *or* a skellington."

I looked at Jenna. "The school burial ground!" I said.

"Yeah," she nodded. "If we knew where it was we could kind of finish off the whole story, couldn't we?"

I began zipping up my hoody. "Come on,

then," I said. "Let's go and find him."

"If we find Billy's grave," Claire said, "can we play funerals?"

The graveyard was very small. Once there had been ornate iron railings around it, but these were practically all rusted away and brambles and ivy had grown through those that remained, twisting and knotting themselves into tight tangles. Within what was left of the railings, nettles and briars grew thickly, hiding the gravestones from view. Luckily, we discovered that the dense undergrowth had partly protected the stones and crosses, and after pulling, dragging and burrowing into the foliage (we got Claire to get some rubber gloves from Scatty) we found no fewer than six small burial stones. And one of these was for Billy.

It read:

Billy Brown. 1906–1916.
Died after a severe illness bravely borne.
Fight the Good Fight

We pulled out some of the nettles from around it and stood and stared at it for some time.

"There's nothing about where he came from," Jenna said at last, "or saying that he's going to be missed by his parents or brothers and sisters."

I shook my head. I didn't say anything because actually I felt a bit choked.

"My grandad said that they sent boys to that school to get rid of them!" Claire put in.

"So perhaps he didn't have any close relatives," I said after a moment.

"Or perhaps he did, and they just didn't care about him," said Jenna.

There was another long silence. "Poor Billy," we both said together.

CHAPTER TWELVE

"So, how much do we tell Mum?" Jenna asked as we walked home.

"Knowing you, you'll blurt out the lot."

"Well, she's bound to find out anyway, because Claire will tell the UFOs and Scatty, and once *she* knows it'll be all over the village."

"Maybe that won't be a bad thing," I said. "If everyone knows what we can do then they'll all bring us their unsolved spooky mysteries."

"Talking of those," Jenna said, frowning, "what about that Victorian woman?"

I shrugged. "Dunno. She obviously hasn't got anything to do with Billy. . ."

Jenna sighed. "There was something funny

about her, you know. She wasn't like the other ghosts."

"How wasn't she?"

"She wasn't ... wasn't..." Jenna's face screwed up with the effort of trying to think and then she gave a sigh. "Oh, I can't explain," she said. "Anyway, you're not really listening to me, are you?"

"Well, I was," I said, stopping dead, "but I've just remembered something. In all that excitement I forgot my football – it's still at Horror House."

"Oh, go back later for it!" Jenna said. "Let's get home and get something decent to eat now. I'm *starving*!"

As we polished off a couple of eggs on toast each we gave Mum a garbled explanation of what had happened. At the end of it she stared at us, puzzled. "I don't know what it is with you two: ghost dogs, skeletons in trunks, boys in baths ... whatever next? Why can't you do normal things?"

"Because we don't live in a normal place!" I said, sticking another couple of slices of bread into the toaster. "It's not our fault we're living in this weird village."

"Where everyone is either barmy or. . ."

"Or buried!" I chipped in, and we both sniggered.

I gave Jenna a look, thinking that we'd better leave it at that. We hadn't told Mum *everything* about our visit to Horror House – certainly not about the waterfall business. We'd just kind of implied that we'd had "a feeling" that there was a secret room above the bedroom where I'd slept, and then discovered that there was.

"It would be much nicer if you took up studying trees or wild flowers or something," Mum said, and of course we didn't even bother to reply to that.

We finished eating and the shop got busy later, so if I wasn't running up ladders getting stuff from top shelves, I was packing boxes or opening doors for people who were quite capable of opening them for themselves. At the back of my mind the whole time was my football. I hated not having it around.

About four o'clock, though, I was pleased to see it coming into the shop carried by Claire. Accompanying her was Mrs UFO who, though it was a hot day, was wearing a thick, fluffy wool cardigan thing, buttoned right up and reaching to the ground. It was a golden brown colour and made her look like a demented bear. Oh yes, she'd definitely come to live in the right place.

Mum was immediately full on. "Mrs Farrington-Ocelot," she said. "How nice to see you again so soon. What can I get you? Bread? Sugar? Anything at the post office today?"

Mrs UFO looked around vaguely, as if she wasn't quite sure where she was.

"I do hope my children weren't any trouble last night," Mum went on, while I relieved Claire of my football.

"Well," said Mrs UFO, suddenly pulling herself together, "they cleared up a little mystery *and* discovered a secret room behind a bookcase."

"Mmm," Mum said, unsure of whether this was a Good Thing or a Bad Thing.

"They've probably told you about it. . . So sad about poor Billy," Mrs UFO trilled on, "but things like that used to happen in those sorts of schools. They were horrid and frightening places! However, we're going to open up the little room now and use it properly. I'm going to turn it into a sewing room and put flowers and pictures in it to make it pretty."

"*What* a good idea!" Mum enthused, though if

Mrs UFO had said she was putting bars across the door to keep lions in there I think she would have said the same, just to be agreeable.

"And such a funny thing," Mrs UFO went on, "the house was very damp – always has been, apparently. But this morning it seems to have dried out completely. It's all most peculiar!"

Jenna and I looked at each other.

"Some funny trait to do with the weather, I suppose. . ."

"Mmm," Mum said. "Now, is there anything I can get you today?"

Mrs UFO glanced outside. "Do you sell umbrellas?"

Mum shook her head. "I'm afraid we don't."

"Because it's getting awfully dark out and I fear it might rain. . ."

We looked out. It *was* getting dark. It was one of those times where suddenly it goes as black as anything and you pretend that the end of the world's coming.

Then it started to rain. We didn't see any lightning, but there was a sudden, huge clap of thunder and after a few big blobs of rain it began pouring down in earnest, lashing across the green and forming instant puddles everywhere.

We all stood in front of the door, looking out. Mum was waffling on about the weather for this time of the year, Mrs UFO was saying how worried she was about getting home, and Claire was doing little dance steps up and down, humming to herself.

Then Jenna, who was right beside the door, suddenly gasped, "Oh!" she said. "She's there! She's coming across the green!"

"Who's there?" Mum said. But I didn't have to ask.

"She's wearing the same yellow dress – and there's blood and everything!"

"*What?*" Mum hurried out from behind the counter, looking concerned, and Mrs UFO, Claire and I all looked out on to the green, in the direction Jenna was staring.

Mrs UFO said, "Oh dear. It looks like there's been an accident!"

Mum said, "What a strange outfit. She's getting soaked!"

Claire said, "Her dress has got all blood on it!"

Jenna turned to me. "Can *you* see her too?"

I nodded, bewildered.

"Is it a ghost?" Claire asked.

"Well, no, it isn't," Jenna said, breathing

fast. "Not if everyone else can see her as well."

The woman was running now, blundering along as if she couldn't make out where she was going. Mud streaked the bottom of her dress. I could see it all for myself now, just as Jenna had described her before.

Mum flung open the door of the shop and the rain gusted in. "Over here!" she called to the woman. "We'll help you!"

And the ghost who was not a ghost burst into tears and stumbled the last few steps into the shop, where she collapsed on to the floor.

Mum had taken charge, calming the woman down, finding dry clothes for her and making a cup of tea, and Mrs UFO, who'd done a course in first aid, had found a clean tea towel and applied it to the woman's head. I'd been instructed to ring 999 for an ambulance, and this had driven to find the woman's husband first, because he was still in the car at the edge of the green where the accident had happened.

As soon as everything was in order and it was clear that no one was badly hurt, Jenna started on the questions. "I hope you don't mind me asking," she said to the woman, "but why are you dressed like that?"

"Well, we were going to a fancy dress party," the woman said, looking down at the bloodied, muddy, yellow dress. She gave an big shiver. "My husband's got the full works, too: Victorian dress suit, wing collar, top hat. We hired them."

"Oh," Jenna breathed.

So not Victorian at all, I thought. *Just dressed like it. . .*

"And how did the accident happen?" Mum asked gently.

"So silly. . . We were having a bit of a row," the woman said. "It suddenly started to get dark and he turned to shout at me, and as he did so we came to a sharp bend in the road. He braked, the car skidded and went into a big oak tree."

And that was why the oak tree had been the same size. . .

I looked at Jenna, who was white as a ghost herself.

She walked away from the little group gathered round the woman and I followed her into the kitchen "You OK?" I asked.

She shook her head. "No, I'm not." She stared at me. "You know what's happened, don't you?"

"Well, kind of," I said. "She wasn't a ghost at all, was she?"

"No, she wasn't. It worked the other way round!" Jenna said, looking at me bleakly. "As if it's not bad enough seeing scenes from the past, I'm now seeing scenes from the *future*."

I didn't reply at first because I knew I wouldn't have fancied it myself. I mean, it might be OK if you're only going to see nice things happening, but I certainly didn't fancy seeing any disasters. "It would be good if you could look ahead and find out if I'm going get into one of the big teams, though," I said.

"Oh, yes, that *would* be good," she said sarcastically. She lowered her voice. "You know, sometimes I wish we weren't psychic."

"Don't be mad. We wouldn't have any ghosts to hunt!" I slapped her on the back. "Tell you what, see if you can predict who'll win the FA Cup."

"Is that all you think about? Oh, do shut up!" she said, and she went off in a huff.

She'll be OK once the next ghost comes along, though. . .

No, she usually answered the other way round," he [illegible] [illegible] [illegible] [illegible] "I'd not had enough [illegible] [illegible] [illegible] new [illegible] [illegible] [illegible]

[illegible] [illegible] that [illegible] I wouldn't [illegible] [illegible] [illegible] it might be OK if you're only [illegible] [illegible] [illegible] [illegible] certainly didn't [illegible] [illegible]

It would be good [illegible] [illegible] [illegible] and [illegible] meeting [illegible] [illegible] [illegible] thought," I said.

"Oh, yes, that would be lovely," she said [illegible] [illegible] [illegible] [illegible] [illegible] [illegible] [illegible] her hand against my [illegible]

"Well [illegible] we wouldn't [illegible] [illegible] on hand," I [illegible] [illegible] the [illegible] you [illegible] [illegible] you can [illegible] you'll [illegible] the Cup."

"Well, if you think [illegible] [illegible] [illegible] [illegible] [illegible] [illegible]

[illegible] OK [illegible] [illegible] [illegible] along smooth.

Look out for more seriously spooky adventures...

HAUNTED HOUSE

When Jake and Jenna move to a village in the middle of nowhere Jake's sure that years of boredom stretch ahead of them. Until Jenna sees the ghost...

From then on Jake and Jenna decide that ghost-hunting will be the new hobby that Mum's always on at them about. Who'd have thought that such a small place could have so many? There's the wandering ghost dog and – much more spooky – the restless spirit that haunts the tumbledown empty house, weeping and wailing. No one knows why it's so sad, but Jake and Jenna are determined to find out – even if it means staying up all night in the dark, deserted, very *haunted* house...

PLAGUE HOUSE

When Jake and Jenna stumble across Corpses' Copse one day, they know there's something very sinister about it. Jenna hears children singing "Ring a Ring o' Roses", the chilling nursery rhyme that dates from the time of the Plague... The villagerswarn the twins to keep away from the copse, but Jenna is sure that a ghost from the past desperately needs her help, and she *can't* say no...